THE SWAMPEES
THE RAREST EGG

BY GILLIAN OSBAND
ILLUSTRATED BY BOBBIE SPARGO

PATTI THE APATOSAURUS

P.T. THE PTERANODON

ELLA THE ELASMOSAURUS

REX THE TYRANNOSAURUS

STIGGY THE STEGOSAURUS

MAX THE WOOLLY MAMMOTH

A GROLIER COMPANY

FRANKLIN WATTS
New York/London/Toronto/Sydney/1982

WELCOME TO SWAMP VALLEY...

Far away is a valley where life has remained unchanged for fifty million years.

This is Swamp Valley, home of the Swampees.

"That's us!"

Meet Max, the leader of the Swampees.

Patti is always ready to help.

Stiggy is the inventor and mission controller.

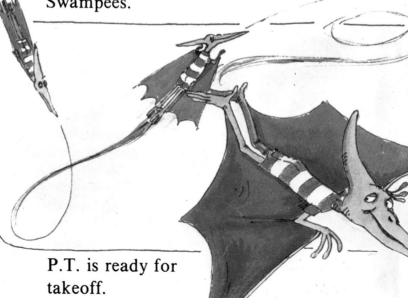

P.T. is ready for takeoff.

And there's never been an
Elasmosaurus like Ella.

Last, but not least, is Rex.

Friends everywhere are
Swampee Scouts.

This is Dr. Croc—the
Swampees' enemy.

He lives in Crocodile
Swamp.

Early one morning, the sounds of hammering filled Swampee Headquarters.

Ella knew what that meant. Stiggy was working on a secret project, and she was going to find out what it was.

Inside the invention room, Stiggy
whistled as he hammered and sawed,
cut and glued.

"Ella knows I'm up to something,"
he said to himself. "But she doesn't
know how *far* up!"

At last Stiggy came out carrying a huge kite.

"I'm going to fly!" Stiggy announced. "Will you help me, Ella?"

Ella sniffed. "Well, I could give a little expert help."

They both raced to the hill.

Ella held tightly to the long string, as Stiggy ran down the hillside.

He ran ... and ran ... until finally a gust of wind caught the kite and lifted him into the air.

Just then P.T. flew by.

"Well, what do you know? A flying Stegosaurus!" he exclaimed. "Hey, Stiggy, can you do this?"

CRRAAAASHHH!!

They weren't hurt, but Stiggy's kite was wrecked.

No one noticed the dark figure scurrying away toward Dr. Croc's Crocodile Swamp.

ARE YOU ALRIGHT?

P.T.'s wing caught the kite string. Before they knew it, they were tangled and headed straight for the treetops.

Meanwhile at Crocodile Swamp, Dr. Croc was
watching the news on television. A group of children
had found the egg of the rarest bird in the world,
the yellow-toed giant crosspatch. They were going
to guard the egg until it hatched.

Just then, Dr. Croc's chief spy burst in. Breathlessly, he told Dr. Croc about all he had seen in Swamp Valley.

"For once, you've brought me a useful report," Dr. Croc said. "Soon I will have the rarest egg in the world."

A few days later, at the nest, the children were guarding the egg.

Rose looked around. Some tiny specks in the sky seemed to be getting larger.

She lifted her binoculars and took a closer look.

"It's Dr. Croc and his evil crocodiles!" she gasped. "I must call the Swampees right away!"

Back in Swamp Valley, Stiggy was cleaning the Swampees' computer. When the Swampee Scrambler rang out, Max answered the Swampee Scout's call.

Max looked serious after he heard the news. "Dr. Croc is heading for the rarest egg in the world—on a kite! What a time for the computer to be out of action!"

"We'll have to use our common sense," said Max.

"P.T. certainly managed to stop me flying," said Stiggy. "All we need is something to tangle up Dr. Croc's kites."

"Balloons!" cried Patti. "If we blow up balloons with helium gas, they will float up and do the job!"

The Swampees collected all the equipment. Balloons, string, and containers of helium gas were loaded onto Rex's Swampship.

By the time Rex arrived at the nest, Dr. Croc was dangerously close.

Rex and the Swampee Scouts worked fast to inflate the balloons and tie them with string.

Suddenly, a gust of wind brought Dr. Croc and his henchmen swooping in.

The balloons burst as the
crocodiles crashed into them. Kite
strings tangled with balloon strings
and down came the crocodiles.

As Dr. Croc stomped away, he ran right into a flour bomb.

"You haven't seen the last of me!" he snarled. "I will get that egg!"

"We need another plan," said Max after Rex had reported in.

"Then why not hide the real egg and put a false egg in its place?" suggested Patti.

"And it would be nice to have a tree that could keep an eye on things," said Max, looking at Ella.

"Disguise *me* as a tree!" said Ella.

Max and Stiggy stayed at Headquarters and the other Swampees set off to help Rex and the Swampee Scouts.

Patti gently moved the real egg and nest to another tree. P.T. helped Ella put on her tree disguise.

The Scouts built a new nest and found an egg-shaped stone. They set up all the traps again around Ella.

Patti painted the stone. Then she balanced the nest in Ella's branches. "Ooh, that tickles," Ella giggled.

"Now we have to wait for Dr. Croc," Patti said.

As night fell, Dr. Croc and his henchmen rustled through the woods. They were disguised as bushes.

Dr. Croc made his way past the traps and finally reached Ella.

"Put the ladder against the tree," Dr. Croc snapped.

Ella could hardly keep still.

Dr. Croc lifted the egg from its nest.

Then, hugging the egg tightly, he climbed down the ladder.

"Let's go!" he said marching off.

Back at Croc Grotto, Dr. Croc held the egg high.

"At last! The rarest egg in the world is mine. Oh, eggs-stasy!" he gloated.

But in his excitement, the egg slipped and fell on his foot with a loud THUD!

Dr. Croc screeched in fury. "This is no egg! I've been swindled!"

Meanwhile, Rex and the
Swampee Scouts were still
guarding the real egg.

Everyone listened. *CRR-R-RACK!*
The egg broke open and out
hopped a tiny yellow-toed giant
crosspatch.

Later at Swamp Valley, the Swampees were having a party. "It's a good thing Patti thought of switching a rock for that egg," P.T. said. "Sort of an eggs-change!"

Max laughed as he wrote in the Swampees' Case Book. "And thanks to the Swampee Scouts, we've saved a rare bird from eggs-tinction!"

BEING A TREE WAS A PRETTY EGGS-HAUSTING EGGS-PERIENCE.

3